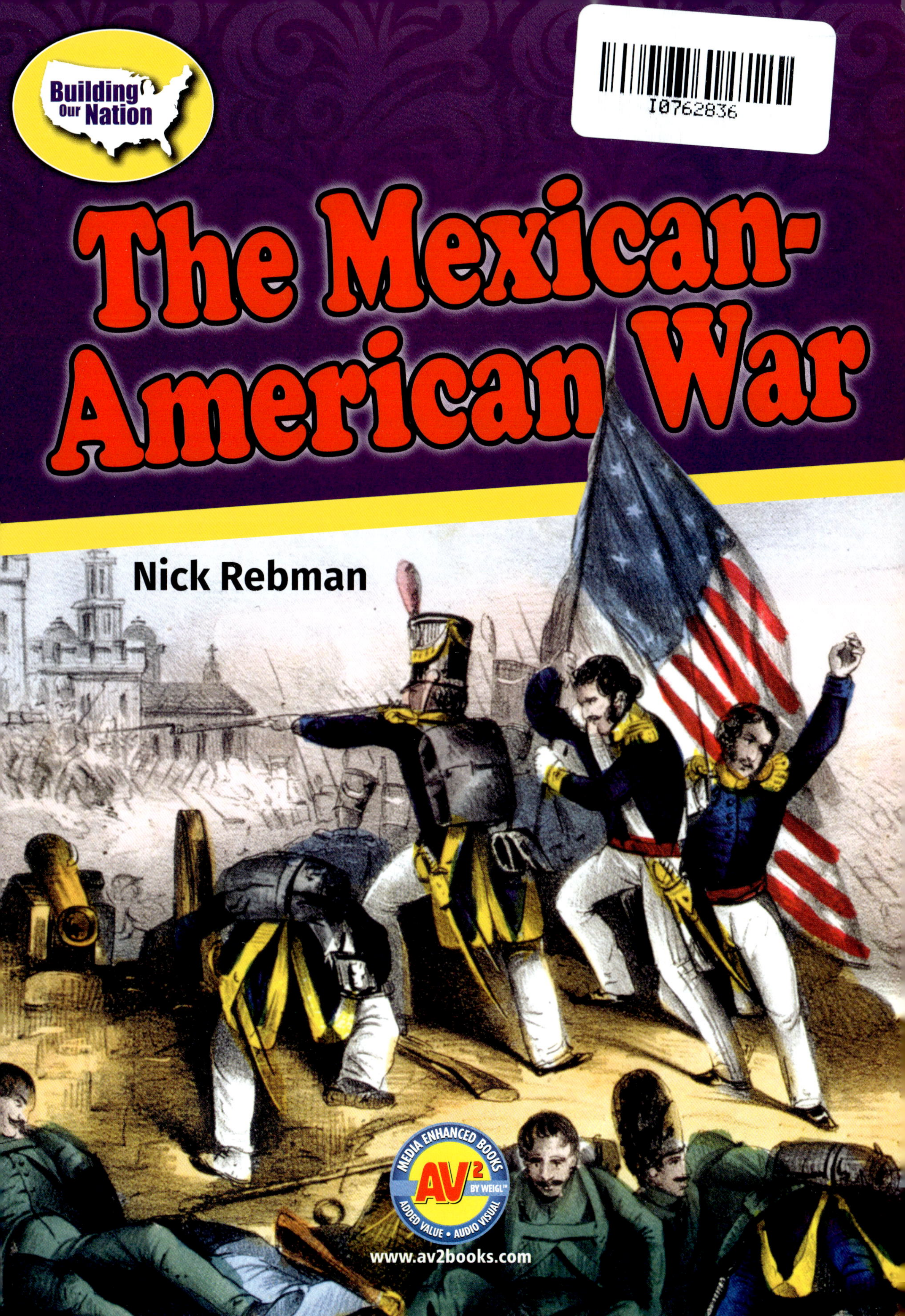
Building Our Nation
I0762836
The Mexican-American War
Nick Rebman
MEDIA ENHANCED BOOKS
AV2 BY WEIGL
ADDED VALUE • AUDIO VISUAL
www.av2books.com

**Go to www.av2books.com, and enter this book's unique code.**

**BOOK CODE**

**AVB42459**

**AV² by Weigl** brings you media enhanced books that support active learning.

AV² provides enriched content that supplements and complements this book. Weigl's AV² books strive to create inspired learning and engage young minds in a total learning experience.

## Your AV² Media Enhanced books come alive with...

**Audio**
Listen to sections of the book read aloud.

**Video**
Watch informative video clips.

**Embedded Weblinks**
Gain additional information for research.

**Try This!**
Complete activities and hands-on experiments.

**Key Words**
Study vocabulary, and complete a matching word activity.

**Quizzes**
Test your knowledge.

**Slide Show**
View images and captions, and prepare a presentation.

**... and much, much more!**

Published by AV² by Weigl
350 5th Avenue, 59th Floor
New York, NY 10118
Website: www.av2books.com



Library of Congress Cataloging-in-Publication Data
Names: Rebman, Nick, author.
Title: The Mexican-American War / Nick Rebman.
Description: New York, NY : AV2 by Weigl, [2020] | Series: Building our nation | Audience: K-3.
Identifiers: LCCN 2018053411 (print) | LCCN 2018054379 (ebook) | ISBN 9781489698841 (Multi User ebook) | ISBN 9781489698858 (Single User ebook) | ISBN 9781489698827 (hardcover : alk. paper) | ISBN 9781489698834 (softcover : alk. paper)
Subjects: LCSH: Mexican War, 1845-1848--Juvenile literature.
Classification: LCC E404 (ebook) | LCC E404 .R39 2020 (print) | DDC 641.5/6362--dc23
LC record available at https://lccn.loc.gov/2018053411

Printed in Guangzhou, China
1 2 3 4 5 6 7 8 9 0  23 22 21 20 19

012019
102318

Project Coordinator: Heather Kissock    Designer: Ana María Vidal

Every reasonable effort has been made to trace ownership and to obtain permission to reprint copyright material. The publishers would be pleased to have any errors or omissions brought to their attention so that they may be corrected in subsequent printings.

Weigl acknowledges Getty Images, Alamy, and Wikimedia as its primary image suppliers for this title.

First published by North Star Editions in 2019.

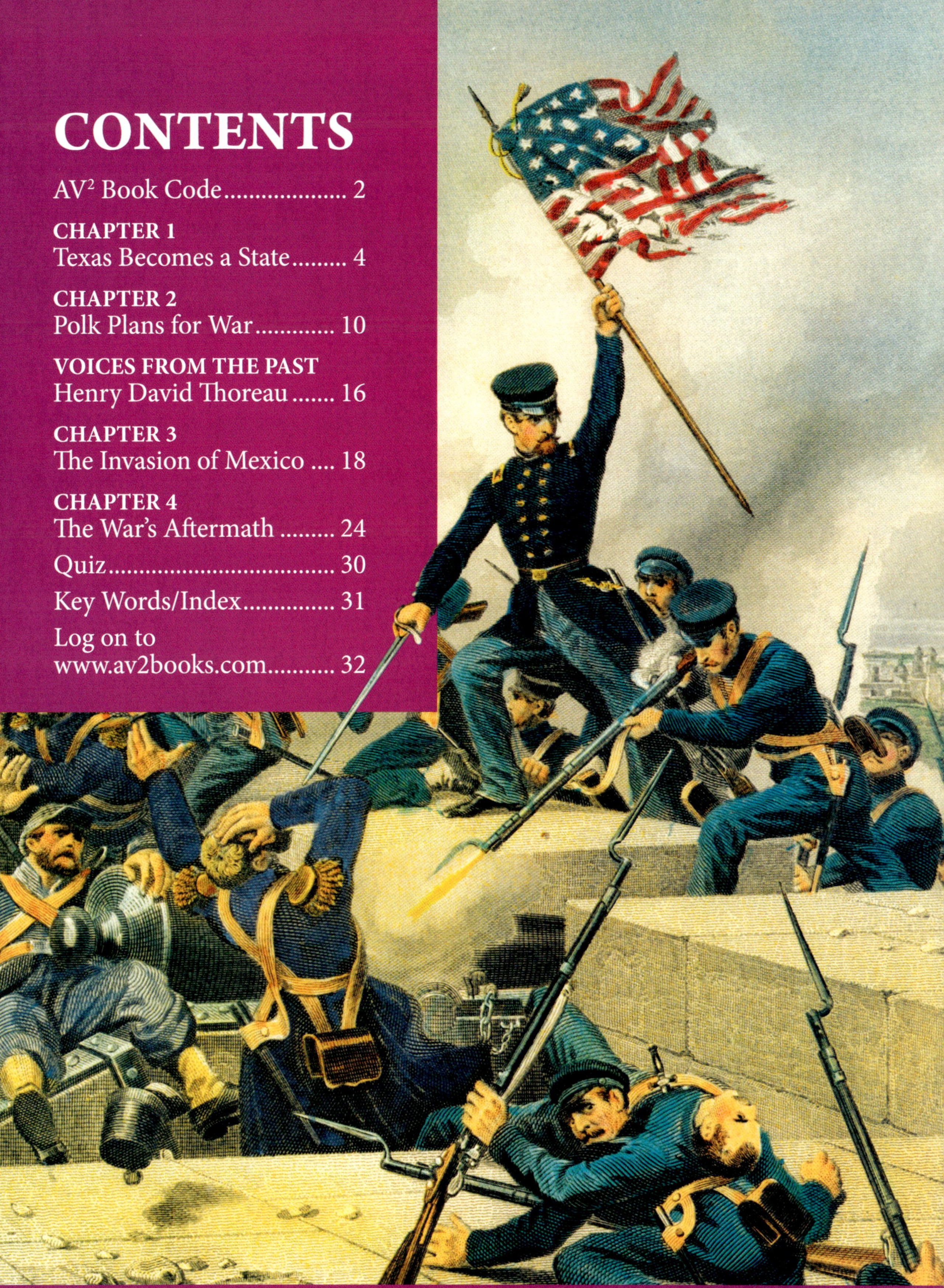

# CONTENTS

Sam Houston was the first president of the Republic of Texas. A hero of the Texas Revolution, he accepted Mexico's surrender following the Battle of San Jacinto.

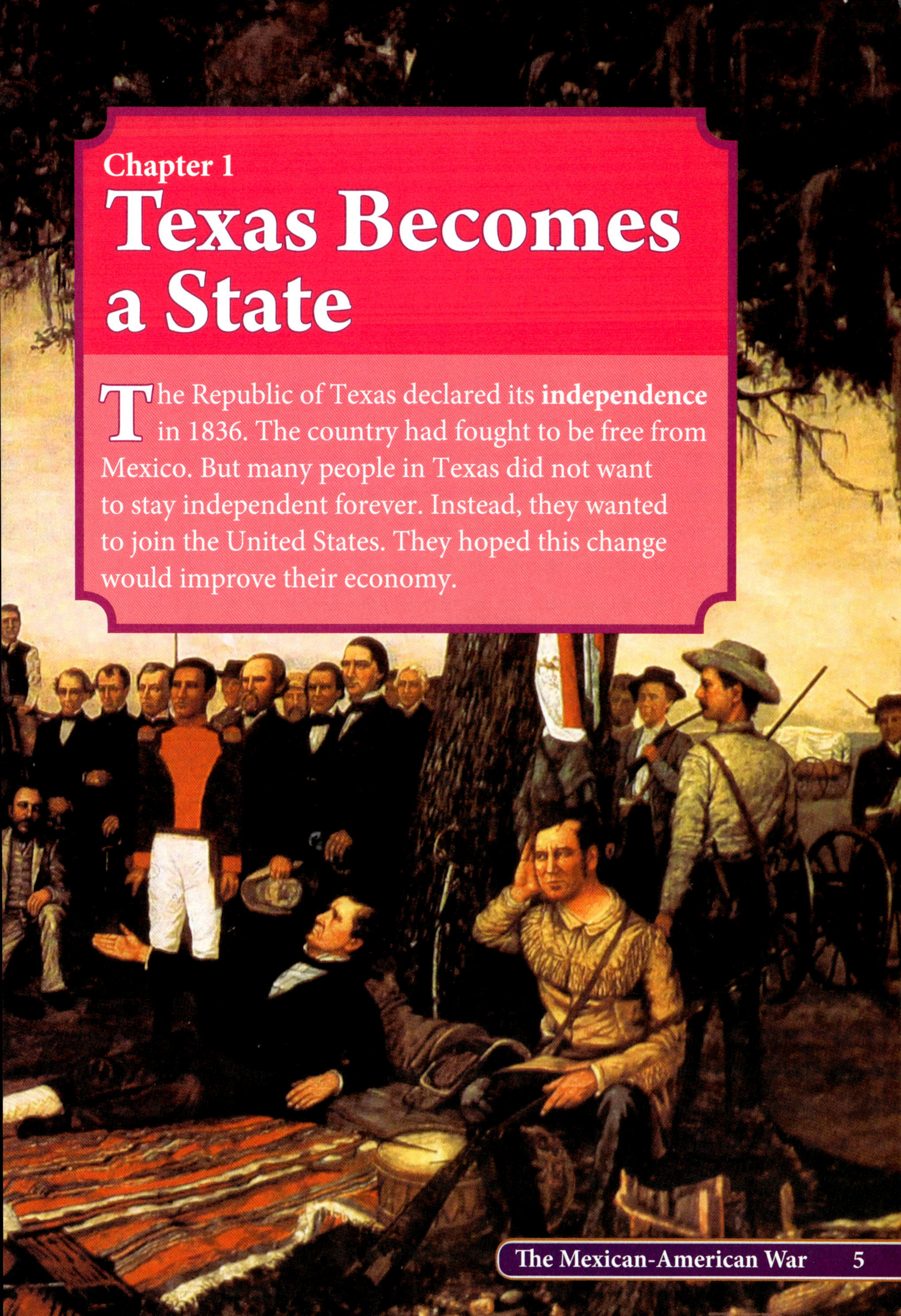

Chapter 1

# Texas Becomes a State

The Republic of Texas declared its **independence** in 1836. The country had fought to be free from Mexico. But many people in Texas did not want to stay independent forever. Instead, they wanted to join the United States. They hoped this change would improve their economy.

However, many U.S. citizens disliked the idea of letting Texas join. They feared Texas would create two major problems.

The first problem involved slavery. At the time, slavery was allowed in half of the states. In the other half, slavery was illegal or being phased out. But the Republic of Texas allowed slavery. And if Texas became a state, there would be more slave states than free states. Many people opposed this idea, especially in northern states.

## Border Dispute

Mexico and the Republic of Texas could not agree on the Republic's borders. Texas felt that the Rio Grande was its southern border. Mexico said that the border was actually the Nueces River. This disagreement was a contributing factor in the Mexican-American War.

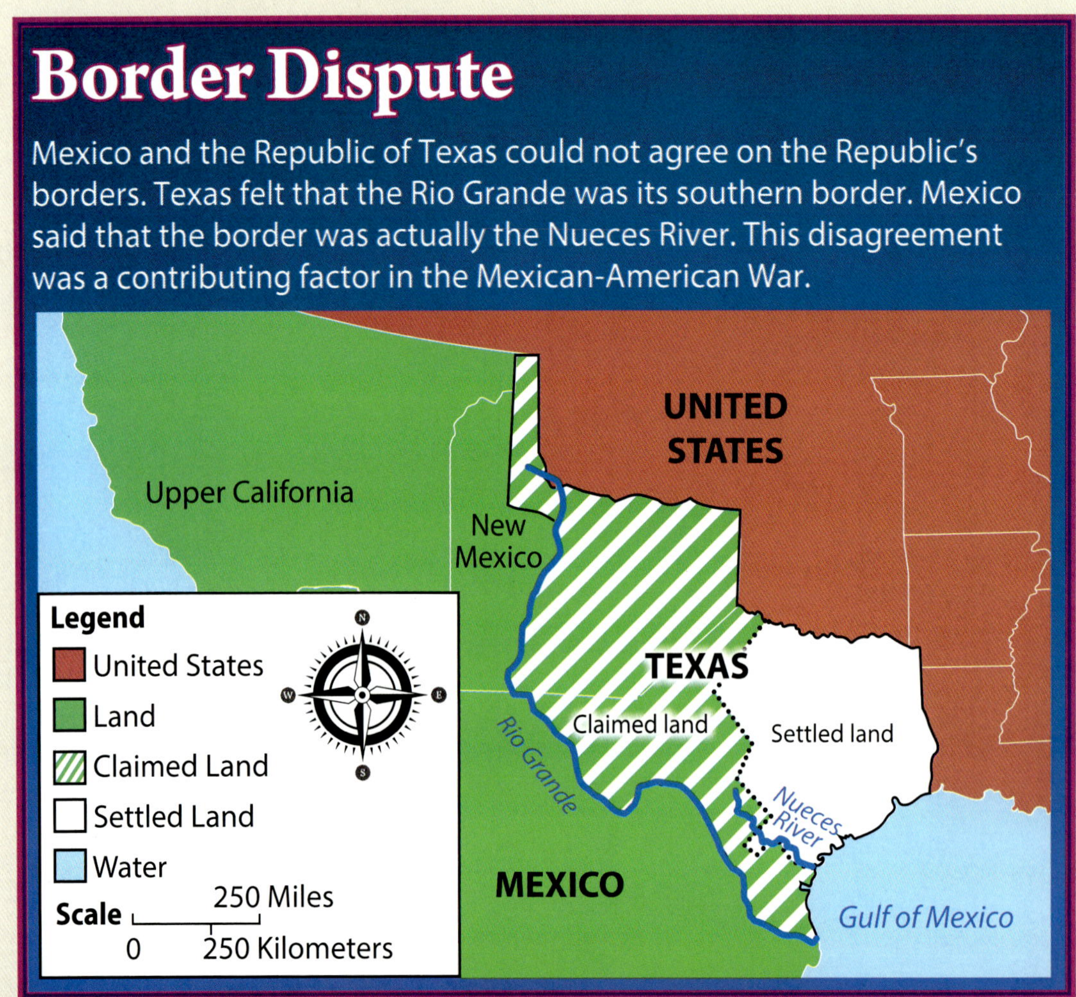

The second problem involved Mexico. Leaders in Mexico did not **recognize** the independence of Texas. They said Texas still belonged to Mexico. For this reason, Mexico would declare war if the United States tried to add Texas. Many U.S. citizens wanted to avoid such a war.

The U.S. Congress debated the topic for months. Finally, in March 1845, the United States agreed to make Texas a state. Mexican leaders were furious when they heard the news. They broke off **relations** with the U.S. government. But despite the earlier threats, Mexico did not declare war.

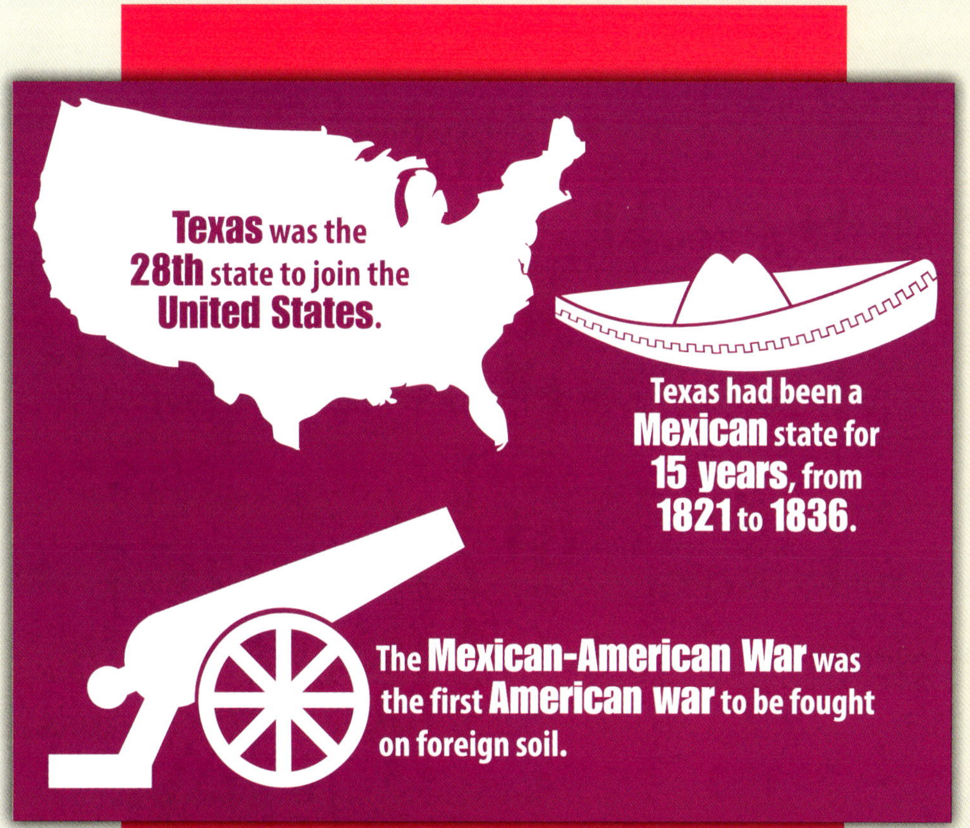

In the summer of 1845, U.S. President James K. Polk sent soldiers to Texas. He wanted to **enforce** his country's claim on the new state. However, Polk had his eyes on more than just Texas. He wanted the United States to expand. With that in mind, he made a secret offer to Mexico. He said the U.S. government would pay for Mexico's northern land. This included the areas of Upper California and New Mexico. Then, Polk waited for a response from the Mexican president.

# Events Leading Up to the War

The Mexican-American War was the culmination of a series of events. As these events unfolded, tension between Mexico and the United States grew.

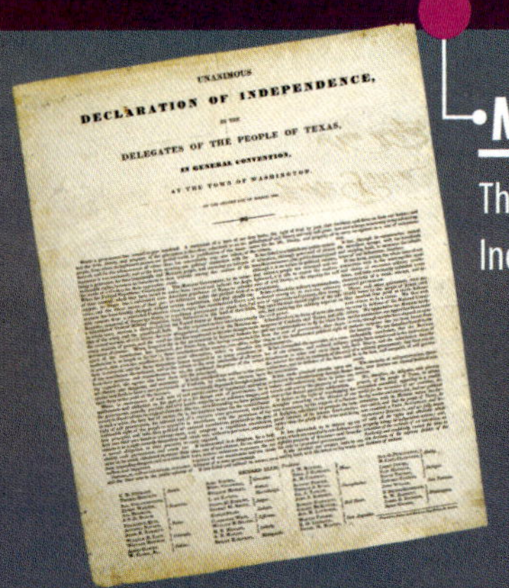
DECLARATION OF INDEPENDENCE,
DELEGATES OF THE PEOPLE OF TEXAS,

**March 2, 1836**

The Texas Declaration of Independence is signed.

**July 4, 1845**

Texas decides to join the United States. Mexico refuses to recognize this union.

**December 29, 1845**

Texas officially joins the United States.

James K. Polk was the U.S. president from 1845 to 1849.

**March 1846**

General Zachary Taylor leads U.S. troops toward the Rio Grande. The United States claims the area east of the river as its territory.

**May 3 to 9,1846**

Mexican forces attack Fort Texas, but the Americans defeat the Mexican army at the Battles of Palo Alto and Resaca de la Palma. The Mexicans are forced to retreat.

**May 13,1846**

Following the Battles of Palo Alto and Resaca de la Palma, Congress declares war on Mexico.

When the U.S. troops first arrived in Texas, they were stationed in Corpus Christi. After Mexico refused to sell its land, the troops were ordered to move closer to the Rio Grande.

Chapter 2

# Polk Plans for War

Polk did not expect Mexico to sell its land to the United States. In fact, the Mexican president didn't even respond to Polk's offer. Even so, Polk was satisfied. He wanted people to think he had tried to solve the issue peacefully. But really, he was planning for war.

In March 1846, approximately 4,000 U.S. soldiers arrived at the Rio Grande. According to the U.S. claim, this river marked the southern border of Texas. But the area was actually controlled by Mexico. Even the U.S. soldiers did not think they had a right to be there. Polk knew that Mexico's leaders would be upset. From their point of view, the United States had invaded Mexico.

Several battles, including the Battle of Palo Alto, took place before the United States actually declared war.

The U.S. soldiers were led by General Zachary Taylor. For nearly a month, Taylor kept his troops near the Rio Grande. Meanwhile, approximately 6,000 Mexican soldiers stood guard on the other side of the river. Mexican general Pedro de Ampudia told Taylor to leave the area. But Taylor refused.

The U.S. Congress officially declared war on Mexico on May 13, 1846.

In April 1846, Mexican troops attacked a group of U.S. soldiers. President Polk finally had what he wanted. Mexico had fired the first shot. Now the United States could go to war.

However, the president does not have the power to declare war. Congress must do it. Some members of Congress hated the idea of war with Mexico. But they were also afraid to vote against it. They feared that people would think they didn't support the U.S. troops. So, most members of Congress voted for the war even if they disagreed with the idea.

Polk expected the war to be fast. After all, the Mexican army had old weapons. Mexico was also low on money. It could not afford a war. In addition, Mexico's government was unstable. In 1846 alone, four different people were president. As a result, the country's leaders could not agree on the best course of action.

Valentin Gomez Farias assumed the role of Mexican president in December 1846, making him the fourth person to hold the job that year.

The war caused a major **controversy** in the United States. Many people supported the conflict. But others were strongly opposed. They blamed Polk for starting an unnecessary war.

Voices From the Past

# Henry David Thoreau

Henry David Thoreau was a poet and writer from Massachusetts. He opposed slavery. He was also against the war with Mexico. In 1846, Thoreau was arrested for not paying taxes. He wanted to make sure "that I do not lend myself to the wrong which I condemn." In other words, Thoreau did not want his tax dollars to be spent on a war he opposed.

If a law "requires you to [cause] injustice to another," he wrote, "then I say, break the law." Thoreau knew he was breaking the law when he did not pay his taxes. But he believed the law was unjust. This behavior is known as civil disobedience.

As punishment for his crime, Thoreau had to spend a night in jail. Even though he did not stop the war, he stood up for what he believed in.

The Battle of Monterrey took place in the fall of 1846. The three-day battle was the first time U.S. soldiers had fought in an urban setting for a prolonged period.

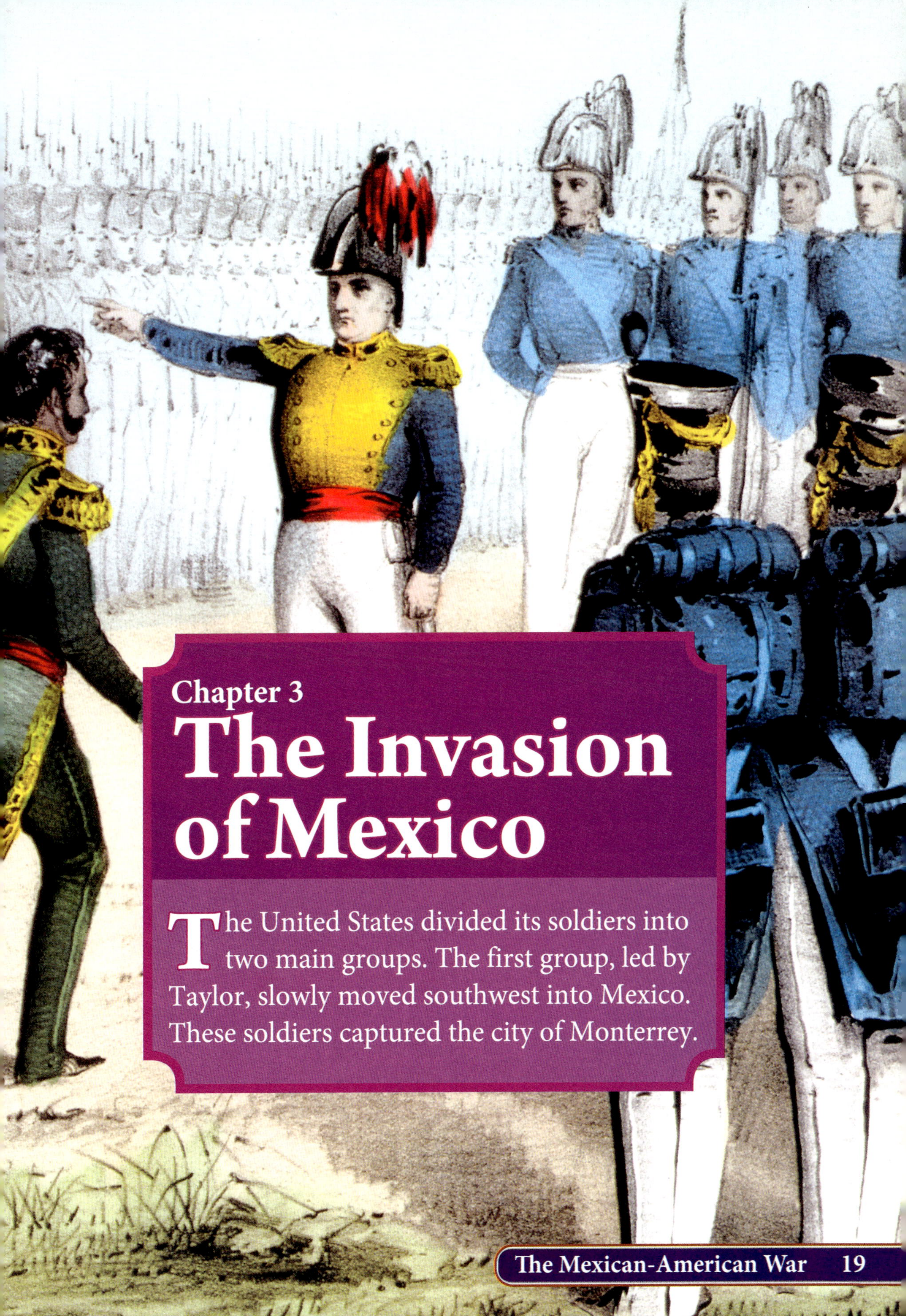

Chapter 3

# The Invasion of Mexico

The United States divided its soldiers into two main groups. The first group, led by Taylor, slowly moved southwest into Mexico. These soldiers captured the city of Monterrey.

General Stephen Watts Kearny captured the territory of New Mexico in August 1846.

The second group was led by General Stephen Watts Kearny. He moved west into New Mexico and Upper California. Parts of this area had a small population. Some of the people who lived there were native to the land. Others were settlers from the United States. And the Mexican citizens who lived there were not treated well by their country's government. For these reasons, Kearny's troops did not face much **resistance**.

Antonio López de Santa Anna led Mexico's troops. Santa Anna was a famous general. He had also been Mexico's president. In February 1847, Santa Anna led his soldiers toward Taylor's troops.

The Mexican army had more soldiers. However, it was poorly organized. And the Mexican soldiers were exhausted from many days of marching. Rather than allowing his soldiers to rest, Santa Anna told them to attack. Taylor's troops held their ground near Monterrey. The fighting was known as the Battle of Buena Vista.

The Battle of Buena Vista lasted from February 22 to February 23, 1847.

Both sides lost hundreds of soldiers. Eventually, Santa Anna decided to retreat. Along the way, many of his soldiers **deserted**.

Mexico lost one battle after another. Even so, the war was not going as quickly as Polk had hoped. For this reason, he sent a third group of U.S. soldiers to Mexico. These troops were led by General Winfield Scott. In March 1847, they took control of Veracruz, a city on Mexico's east coast. From there, they continued on to Mexico City, the nation's capital.

The U.S. soldiers reached Mexico City in August 1847. Scott and Santa Anna signed a temporary **truce**. But peace did not last. Santa Anna did not agree to the United States' terms. So, Scott ordered his troops to attack the city. By September, the U.S. soldiers had taken control. A few minor battles took place in the weeks that followed. But Mexico was defeated.

On September 12, Scott attacked Chapultepec Castle, on the outskirts of Mexico City. When the fortress fell to U.S. forces, the Mexican government had no choice but to surrender.

Taylor's military victory helped him become president. He served in the position from March 1849 until his death in July 1850.

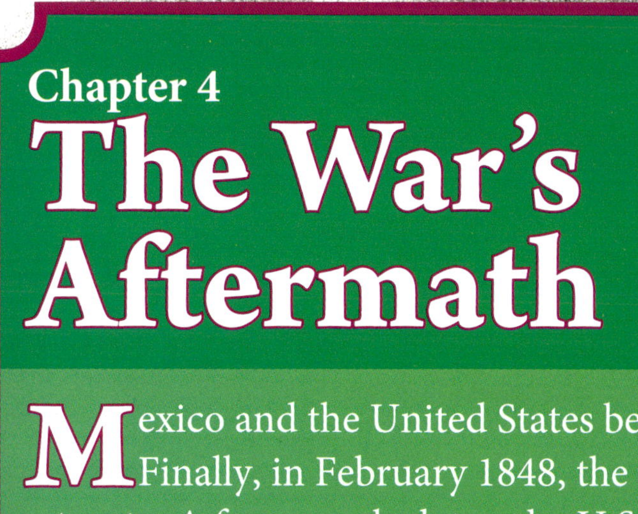

Chapter 4

# The War's Aftermath

Mexico and the United States began peace talks. Finally, in February 1848, the two sides signed a **treaty**. A few months later, the U.S. soldiers left Mexico and returned home. When Taylor got back to the United States, he was a national hero. In November 1848, he was elected president.

The Mexican-American War resulted in many deaths. Approximately 1,700 U.S. soldiers died in battle. And more than 10,000 U.S. soldiers died because of disease. The Mexican army lost 5,000 soldiers in battle. Others were killed by disease. Thousands of Mexican **civilians** died as well. In total, as many as 25,000 Mexicans might have died during the war.

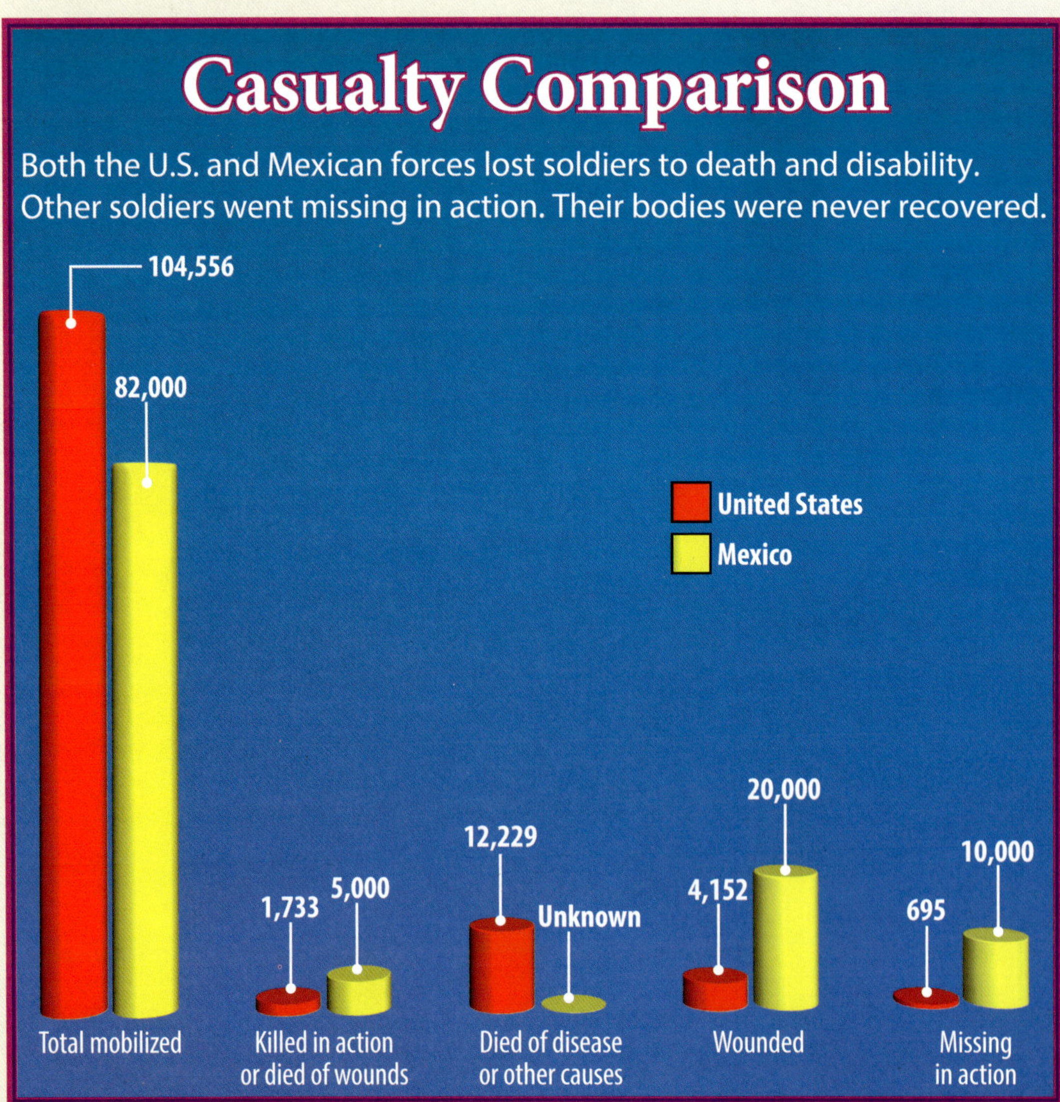

As part of the peace treaty, Mexico agreed that Texas was part of the United States. However, Mexico gave up much more than just Texas. The treaty also required Mexico to sell Upper California and New Mexico to the United States. This was the land that Polk had wanted to buy before the war started. But this time, the United States paid much less.

The Mexican citizens living in Upper California and New Mexico were now on U.S. land. According to the treaty, they were allowed to become U.S. citizens.

However, they did not receive equal rights for several years. The Native Peoples who lived on these lands were treated even worse. The U.S. government did not give them any rights at all.

In time, the new U.S. land was divided into several states. They included California, Nevada, Utah, Arizona, and New Mexico. The land also became parts of Wyoming, Colorado, Kansas, and Oklahoma.

The United States had gained a huge amount of land. But one topic still divided the nation. U.S. citizens could not agree on slavery. In the South, many people wanted the new territory to allow slavery. In the North, most people opposed this idea. They did not want more slave states to join. Angry debates divided the two halves of the country. By the 1860s, the arguments turned violent. Slavery would become one of the causes of the U.S. Civil War (1861–1865).

People traveled along the Santa Fe Trail to settle in the southwestern United States.

# Gains in U.S. Territory (1848)

The Mexican-American War had profound effects on the history of the United States. Its acquisition of new lands led to more settlements and the creation of new states.

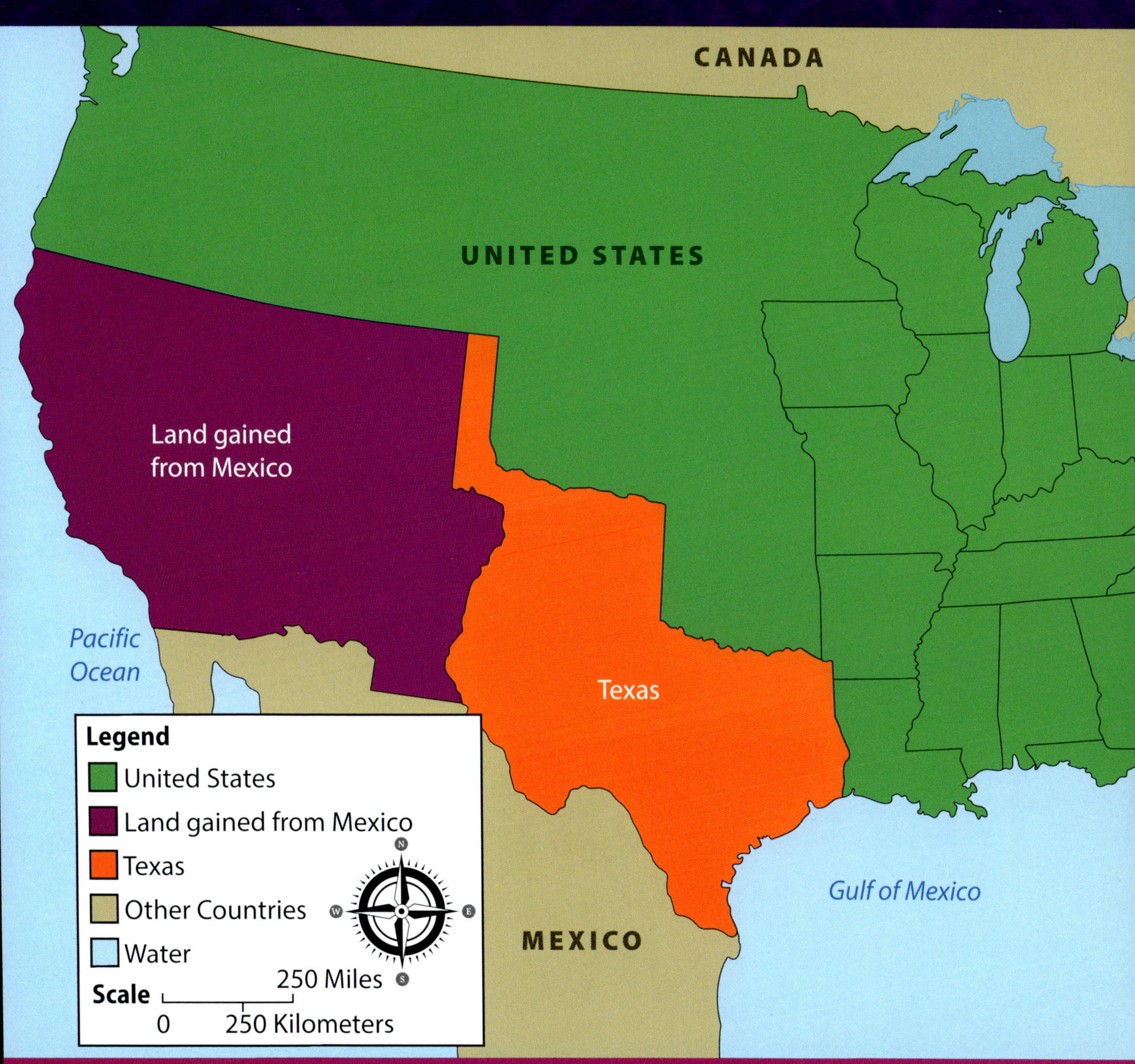

# Quiz

**1** In what year did the Republic of Texas declare its independence?

**2** For how long had Texas been a Mexican state?

**3** Who was the U.S. president during the Mexican-American War?

**4** Who led the U.S. troops to the Rio Grande in 1846?

**5** When did the U.S. Congress officially declare war on Mexico?

**6** Who led Mexico's troops?

**7** When did U.S. troops reach Mexico City?

**8** How much land did Mexico cede to the United States under the peace treaty?

**Answer: 1.** 1836 **2.** 15 years **3.** James K. Polk **4.** General Zachary Taylor **5.** May 13, 1846 **6.** Antonio López de Santa Anna **7.** August 1847 **8.** 525,000 square miles (1.36 million sq. km)

# Key Words

**civilians:** people who are not in the military

**controversy:** a topic or event that causes much disagreement

**deserted:** left an army without permission

**enforce:** to make sure something happens

**independence:** the ability to make decisions without being controlled by another government

**recognize:** to officially agree that something is true or legal

**relations:** the act of two countries or groups speaking to each other

**resistance:** the act of fighting back

**treaty:** an official agreement between groups

**truce:** an agreement to stop fighting for a period of time

# Index

# Log on to www.av2books.com

AV² by Weigl brings you media enhanced books that support active learning. Go to www.av2books.com, and enter the special code found on page 2 of this book. You will gain access to enriched and enhanced content that supplements and complements this book. Content includes video, audio, weblinks, quizzes, a slide show, and activities.

## AV² Online Navigation

**Audio**
Listen to sections of the book read aloud.

**Book Pages**
AV² pages directly correspond to pages in the book.

**Video**
Watch informative video clips.

**Embedded Weblinks**
Gain additional information for research.

**Key Words**
Study vocabulary, and complete a matching word activity.

**Try This!**
Complete activities and hands-on experiments.

**Quizzes**
Test your knowledge.

**Slide Show**
View images and captions, and prepare a presentation.

**AV² was built to bridge the gap between print and digital. We encourage you to tell us what you like and what you want to see in the future.**

**Sign up to be an AV² Ambassador at www.av2books.com/ambassador.**

Due to the dynamic nature of the Internet, some of the URLs and activities provided as part of AV² by Weigl may have changed or ceased to exist. AV² by Weigl accepts no responsibility for any such changes. All media enhanced books are regularly monitored to update addresses and sites in a timely manner. Contact AV² by Weigl at 1-866-649-3445 or av2books@weigl.com with any questions, comments, or feedback.